~~Goodear~~

Goodyear

Petunia Pepper's ★ Picture Day ★

Written by **Cathy Breisacher**   Pictures by **Christian Elden**

To Chuck, Mom, and in memory of Dad—
You are my picture of love and encouragement.

Warner Press Kids™
educate • nurture • inspire
www.warnerpress.org

79425017408

Text © 2010 by Cathy Breisacher
Illustrations by Christian Elden © 2010 Warner Press
ISBN: 978-1-59317-397-5

Published by Warner Press, Inc, 1201 E. 5th Street, Anderson, IN 46012

Design Layout: Curtis Corzine   Editors: Robin Fogle, Karen Rhodes

---

Library of Congress Cataloging-in-Publication Data

Breisacher, Cathy.
   Petunia Pepper's picture day / by Cathy Breisacher ; illustrated by Christian Elden.
      p. cm.
   Summary: Every year something spoils Petunia's school picture, and
this year is no exception as she misses the school bus, gets rained on,
slides into a hot dog vendor's cart, and more. Includes a page entitled
"Take Time Out for God's Word."
   ISBN 978-1-59317-397-5
   [1. Photographs--Fiction. 2. Schools--Fiction. 3. Christian
life--Fiction.] I. Elden, Christian, ill. II. Title.
   PZ7.B7487Pe 2010
   [E]--dc22
                              2010009001

Printed in Mexico

Petunia Pepper

wanted to look perfect for Picture Day.

Each year, her mom proudly placed Petunia's school picture on the piano in the parlor.

In her preschool picture, Petunia had
puffy hair, which looked like a powder puff.

In her kindergarten picture, Petunia was missing her front teeth. Her smile made her look like a pumpkin.

In first grade, Petunia had pink eye.
Her right eye was puffy and pinched shut.

Poor Petunia Pepper.

For three years, no one wanted a copy of Petunia's picture except her mom, dad and grandma.

"You have personality," said her dad.
"You always look pretty," added her mom.
"My precious Petunia, you look like me," said Grandma Pepper.

"This year I'm going to have a picture *everyone* wants," Petunia said.

On Picture Day, Petunia woke early. She painted her nails, placed a ribbon in her hair and slipped into her polished shoes. Then she paraded through the house like a princess.

"You look peachy," said Petunia's dad.
"Perfect," said her mom.
"Better hurry up and eat your pancakes,"
said Grandma Pepper.

Petunia gobbled up her food, but she spilled a drop of syrup on her lap. She dabbed it off with water, then dashed out of the house toward the bus stop.

But the bus pulled away from the curb seconds before Petunia reached it.
Poor Petunia Pepper! Now she would have to walk to school.

Petunia peered at the sky. Puffy gray clouds covered the sun. *Plink, plunk*. A few raindrops dotted the sidewalk. She picked up her pace.

Petunia dashed through the park and past the playground. *Plop!* She slipped on a banana peel in the overgrown grass and landed on the pavement.

Poor Petunia Pepper!

She brushed the dirt off of her dress and hurried on her way. "Can't stop now," she mumbled. "I'll be late for Picture Day."

Petunia ran faster but her polished shoes were slippery.
She noticed a hot dog vendor on the street corner,
preparing for the day. She tried to slow down, but—

—it was too late.

Poor Petunia Pepper!

Mustard and ketchup splattered her dress. A jar of pickles poured over her shoes.

Petunia wiped the stains and plucked the pickles out of her shoes. "Can't stop now," she said to the vendor. "I'll be late for Picture Day."

Petunia had two blocks to go when she heard an old lady screaming.

"My puppy's running away! Someone please help!"

Petunia spotted a poodle on a leash, zigzagging between the cars on the road. Petunia ran after him. She plodded through a puddle, tripped on a pothole and plowed into a freshly painted sign.

Petunia pounced on top of the poodle.

A policeman directing traffic motioned for cars to pull over.
Townspeople gathered around her.

Petunia pouted. "Oh, no! I'm late for Picture Day."

"Don't worry. I'll get you to school on time," the policeman said. He gave her a piggyback ride to his car.

When Petunia arrived at school, Miss Patterson gasped. "Petunia Pepper! You are a mess! You can't have your picture taken looking like that!"

Poor Petunia Pepper!

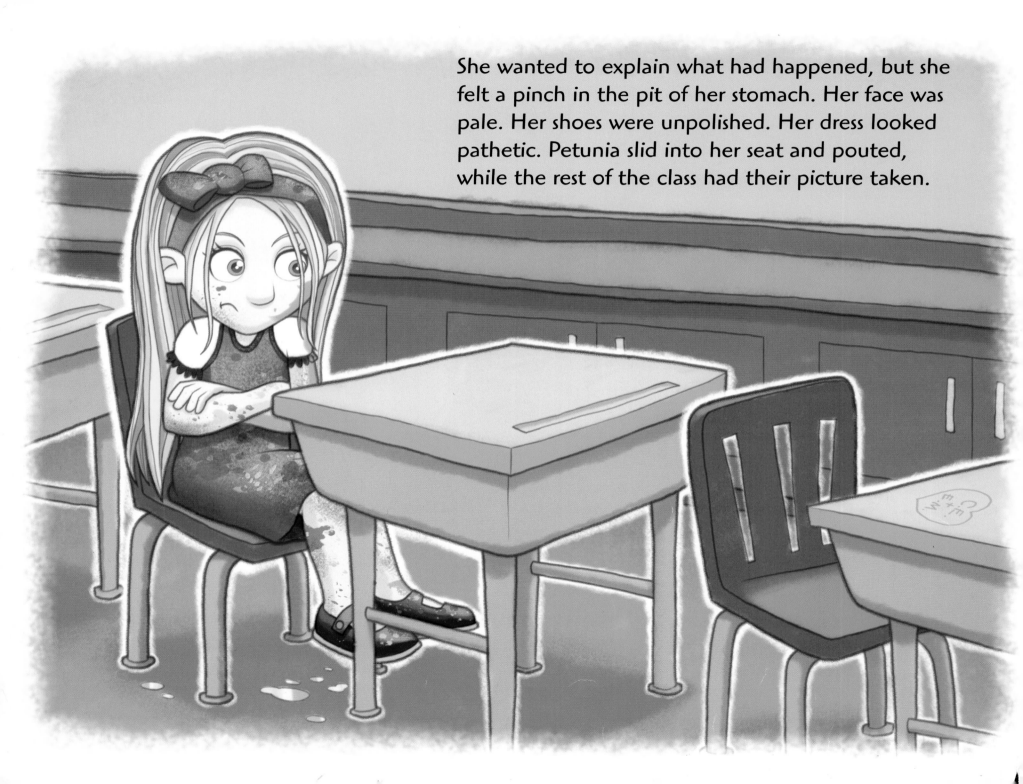

She wanted to explain what had happened, but she felt a pinch in the pit of her stomach. Her face was pale. Her shoes were unpolished. Her dress looked pathetic. Petunia slid into her seat and pouted, while the rest of the class had their picture taken.

MISS
PATTERSON'S
CLASS

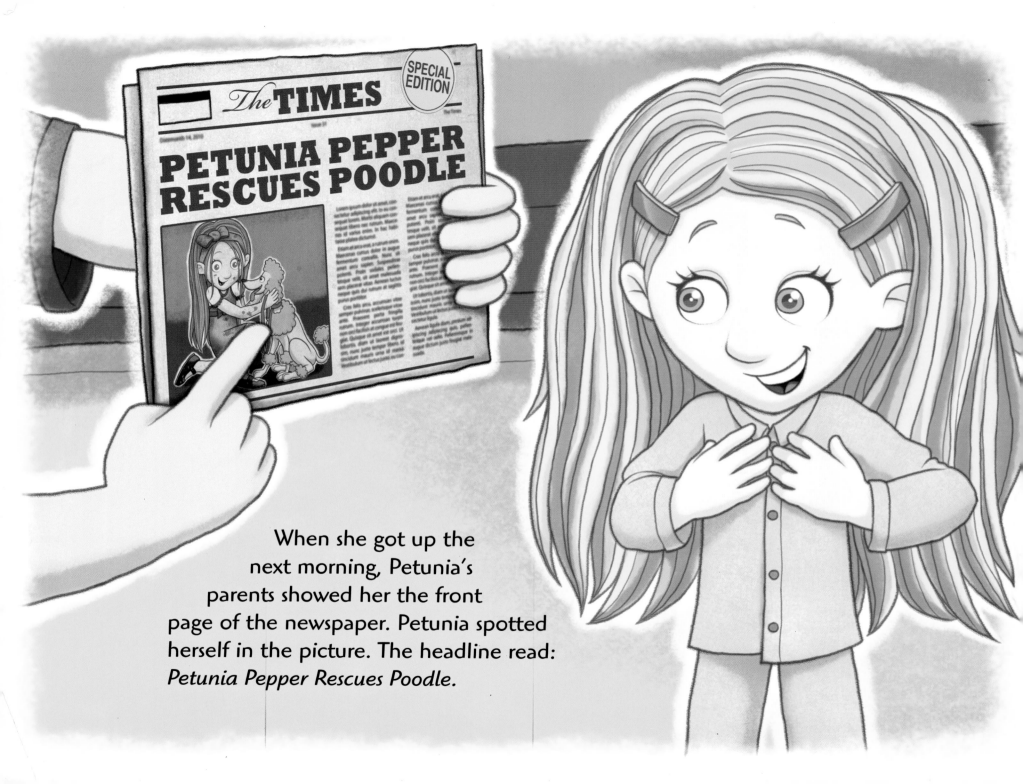

When she got up the next morning, Petunia's parents showed her the front page of the newspaper. Petunia spotted herself in the picture. The headline read: *Petunia Pepper Rescues Poodle.*

"You make the Peppers proud," said Dad.

"You're a hero," said Mom.

"She's just like me," said Grandma Pepper.

Petunia perked up. Then she folded the paper and placed it in her pocket.

At school, each boy and girl in the classroom had a copy of the paper for Petunia to sign.

And Petunia proudly wrote on each paper:

Take Time Out for God's Word

Like Petunia Pepper, maybe you sometimes wish you looked different. Maybe you would like your hair to be longer or straighter. Maybe you want to be taller or shorter. Perhaps you wish you had freckles or wish you didn't.

But, God loves you just the way you are because He made you! Do you know what the Bible tells us about God's love? Here are some Bible verses just for you.

> *For you created my inmost being; you knit me together in my mother's womb. I praise you because I am fearfully and wonderfully made; your works are wonderful, I know that full well.* Psalm 139:13-14 (NIV)
>
> *See, I have engraved you on the palms of my hands; your walls are ever before me.* Isaiah 49:16 (NIV)
>
> *Keep me as the apple of your eye; hide me in the shadow of your wings.* Psalm 17:8 (NIV)
>
> *For we are God's workmanship, created in Christ Jesus to do good works, which God prepared in advance for us to do.* Ephesians 2:10 (NIV)

You are wonderfully made! You are written on His hand! You are the apple of His eye! You are God's workmanship! He made you and He loves you the way you are.

So, the next time you pass out your school picture or your parents hang your picture on the wall, remember that God adores you. Everyday *can* be picture day because you are special and you belong to Him.

That's something to smile about!